A couple of years ago when my son was nine, he got lost. He and I and a crowd of thousands were at Darling Harbour, where there were bands playing and acrobats on stilts and people making passionate speeches. My son darted off to see a man juggling flaming swords and when he looked back, everything had changed. There were only strangers, masses of them, where I used to be.

He was lost for just seven minutes. It was the worst seven minutes of his life, he tells me. It was the worst seven minutes of my life, I can tell you. And when I told my mother, his Grandma, she said the only reason it wasn't the worst seven minutes of her life was because here we all were now sitting safely together on the sofa, eating her banana cake.

But I saw that little smile as Grandma Barbara gazed fondly at her grandson. I'm very familiar with that smile; it means a story is brewing. Poor Tashi was in for another adventure, I knew it. He was going to get lost in a crowd. And not just for seven minutes. There would be acrobats, all right, and music, but there would also be some very, very bad men...

ANNA FIENBERG

Anna and Barbara Fienberg write the Tashi stories together, making up all kinds of daredevil adventures and tricky characters for him to face. Lucky he's such a clever Tashi.

Kim Gamble is one of Australia's favourite illustrators for children. Together Kim and Anna have made such wonderful books as *The Magnificent Nose and Other Marvels*, *The Hottest Boy Who Ever Lived*, the *Tashi* series, the *Minton* picture books, *Joseph*, and a full colour picture book about their favourite adventurer, *There once was a boy called Tashi*.

First published in 2004
This edition first published in 2006

Allen & Unwin
83 Alexander St
Crows Nest NSW 2065
Australia
Phone: (61 2) 8425 0100
Fax: (61 2) 9906 2218
Email: info@allenandunwin.com
Web: www.allenandunwin.com

National Library of Australia
Cataloguing-in-Publication entry:

Fienberg, Anna.
    Tashi lost in the city.

    New cover ed.
    For primary school children.
    ISBN 978 1 74114 963 0.

    ISBN 1 74114 963 0.

    1. Children's stories, Australian. 2. Tashi (Fictitious character) – Juvenile
    fiction. I. Fienberg, Barbara. II. Gamble, Kim. III. Title. (Series: Tashi; 11).

A823.3

Cover and series design by Sandra Nobes
Typeset in Sabon by Tou-Can Design
Printed in Australia by McPhersons Printing Group

10 9 8 7 6 5 4 3 2 1

Tashi

LOST in the CITY

written by
Anna Fienberg
and
Barbara Fienberg

illustrated by
Kim Gamble

ALLEN&UNWIN

'This lift is stuck,' said Jack. He pushed
the ground floor button again. Nothing
happened. Sweat prickled his forehead.

Tashi put his hand on Jack's shoulder.
'Don't worry, we're in a big mall. Someone
will find us soon. All we have to do is sit
and wait.'

Jack could hear his heart thumping.
'I don't like being shut in small places.
Especially when no one knows where we
are,' he added quietly.

Tashi sat on the floor and pulled Jack
after him.

'And I'm *busting*,' whispered Jack.

'Take five deep breaths,' said Tashi,
'and think about something else.'

Jack looked at the great steel doors.
'I wish I'd gone to the toilet *before* we
went to see the skateboards. If only
we had a piece of ghost cake we could
pass right through those doors,
easy peasy –'

'You know,' said Tashi, stretching out
his legs, 'this reminds me of a time I was
trapped in a dark cellar by a man with a
glass eye and a dagger in his belt.'

Jack sat up straight. 'Did the eye look
real?'

'No,' Tashi shook his head. 'It was more like a marble, with a black pupil painted on like a bullseye. But it was the other eye that scared me. Cold and mean and deadly, like a shark's.'

'Gosh,' said Jack. 'How did you escape?'

'Well, it was like this,' Tashi began. 'It was the year our village had a really good harvest. To celebrate, Grandma decided to take me to the city with her to help buy the family's New Year presents. Little Aunt said we could borrow her cart and horse, Plodalong.'

'Was the city a long way from your
village?'

'Oh yes,' nodded Tashi. 'We had to set
out at first light. By late morning we were
in the teeming cobbled streets of the city.
Oh Jack, I'd never seen anything so

4

wonderful. My head swivelled from side
to side. I didn't know where to look first.
There were stalls of candied apples and
roasted ears of corn and silvery fish in
tanks.'

'I hardly had time to glimpse the curio
shops and the bookstalls before we had
to duck our heads under silk banners
announcing family weddings and births.
And the *noise* – everything was so
much louder than in my village.'

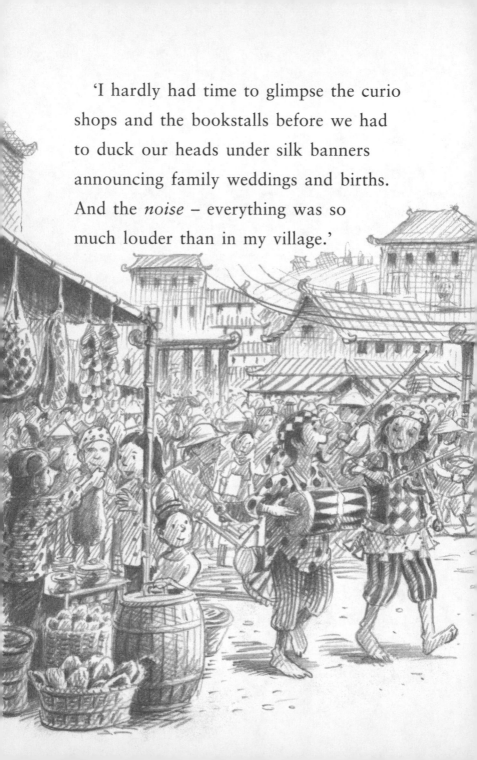

'Street hawkers were calling out their medicines, and stallholders beckoned us to see their toys. And all the time the air thrummed with violins and the drums of street musicians.'

'Is this where you met the man with the glass eye?'

'Not yet,' said Tashi. 'First we had to leave the horse and cart with an old friend of Grandfather's, and then we dived into the crowd.

'"We'll have to be careful, Tashi," said Grandma, "or our money will drip from our hands like water."

'But the very next minute, she couldn't resist a singing cricket in a bamboo cage and then she saw a beautiful music box – just the thing for my mother. Grandma wanted a second box for Third Aunt, but the stallholder said this was the last one. He could get another by four o'clock that afternoon if she wanted it. So we arranged to come back then and I walked on, not realising that Grandma had stopped at another stall to taste some delicious chicken feet.

'I was looking at the hills above the
city – the sun was striking the white walls
of the palace at the top – and the light
was almost blinding. I turned to ask
Grandma if this was the famous Palace
of Expanding Joyfulness, or was it the
Pavilion of Perfect Harmony? But she was
no longer beside me.

'"Grandma!" I called. "GRANDMA!"

'Acrobats moved on to the road, and strangers rushed past, pushing and shouting. But there was no Grandma. I hurried back to the place I'd last seen her. Still no sign of her. I raced up and down the street looking in doorways and behind stalls. I couldn't breathe properly. How quickly everything changed from excitement one minute to being lost and alone the next.'

'Yes!' murmured Jack. 'I know what you mean.'

'Well, as I made my way through the press of people, I heard a commotion and cries of "Mad dog! Mad dog!" Suddenly, as the crowd parted, I saw a big brown dog, foam frothing from its mouth. People were running in all directions like beads scattered on a path, but the dog was chasing a little girl, attracted by her piercing screams. Quick! What to do?

'Through the open gate of a courtyard nearby I spied a sheet hanging on a rail. I ran in and whipped it off.

'The dog was nearly upon the girl,
but it stopped when I drew near with
my arms wide open, hidden by the sheet.
I flung the sheet over the dog, bundled it
up and popped a clothes basket over it.

'The girl's mother was thanking me when the stalls around us began to shake. The road shuddered beneath our feet like something alive. The house with the clothesline collapsed, and the one next to it. People were screaming again. And then, as quickly as it had started, the trembling stopped. The world was still, as if holding its breath. There was complete silence – until we were all startled by cries coming from the collapsed houses. People were buried alive in there! Some folk rushed over and pulled beams and bricks away. Just when everyone thought it was safe, I heard a faint cry from the back of the second house. I lifted a broken screen and saw the head of a man poking out from a mound of rubble. A large rat was investigating his nose.

'A wall beside him looked as if it might fall, but I threw a brick at the rat and called for help. As I worked at the wood and bricks, I looked into the man's baleful eyes –'

'Aha!' cried Jack. 'Bullseye!'

'Yes. One eye was darting angrily all around but the other was fixed straight ahead. A shiver ran through me. Not a word passed between us but I thought, "This is a bad man."

'A few people heard my cries and
came to help. When the man was able
to scramble out of the rubble, he dusted
himself off and said curtly, "I suppose
you want a reward."

'I stiffened. "I don't need one."

'"Just as well," the man snapped, and
without another word, he strode off
through the crowds.

'My legs were trembling. "Wah!" I thought, "I've had enough of this city. If only I could find Grandma and go home."

'Just then a kindly looking stranger stopped beside me and I asked if he had noticed a little old lady carrying a bamboo cage. The gentleman clapped his hands. "Yes, I have. She just went around the corner here." And he led me into an alley.

'The alley was empty and dark. A smell of old garbage and sour wine seeped from the shadows between the buildings. "Tch," said the man, "she must have gone into Beggars Lane. We'll soon find her."

'He took me by the arm and pulled me along to a dilapidated house. *Lucky Chance Hotel* was painted over the door in peeling letters. I was really feeling uneasy about this man and was trying to think of a polite way to leave when he tightened his grip on me. His long sharp fingernails dug into my wrist. He hustled me into the house and shoved me downstairs into a cellar. I scrambled back to the door, too late. The lock clicked. "Why do I ever leave home without a ghost cake?" I groaned.

'I closed my eyes for a moment to get used to the dark. When I opened them, I saw some straw matting, a broken chair and a boy cowering in the corner. "Who is that man?" I asked the tearful boy. "What does he want with us?"

'"He's going to sell us to work in the salt mines," sniffed the boy, "and that'll be the end of us. My father worked there once, before he escaped. He said children were lucky to last a year."

'I shuddered. We told each other our names, and we wandered over to the barred window. Standing on tiptoe, we could see a bit of footpath. I broke the glass with my shoe and together we called, "Help! Help!" but the alley was deserted. No one came by and our throats grew hoarse. Wang slumped to the floor and began to cry again in disappointment. I put my hands over my ears. "Be quiet now, Wang. I'm thinking."

'Wang bit his lip. "Are you thinking of a way to escape? Look around, you can see – there isn't any way."

'"There's always a way if you stay calm and think hard enough," I told him firmly.

'Wang kept up a hopeful silence for another few minutes before he confided, "I'm glad you are here, Tashi. It's better with two, isn't it?"

'I smiled and nodded but I couldn't agree. I thought it was better being alone and lost in the streets than here, waiting to work in the salt mines.

'I stood holding the window bars in the comforting warmth of the sun and noticed how it sparkled on the pieces of broken glass. Yes! Maybe that would work. I tore off a piece of peeling wallpaper and held a shard of glass over it.

'Wang looked on curiously. "What are you doing?"

'"Come and see."

'Using Wang's jacket, I fanned the smoke out through the broken window. The house remained silent. My heart began to thud. Smoke was thickening all around us. I told Wang to pull his shirt up over his nose and mouth. My eyes were streaming and every time I breathed, my throat stung. Oh, maybe I'd done the worst thing – maybe we'd finish up being smoked like pieces of pork! Then we heard shouts and the sound of running footsteps.

'"Quick!" I grabbed Wang's arm. "Come over here against the wall."

'We were just in time. The door burst open and two men ran in and began to beat the flames with their coats. They didn't see us behind the door. Wang and I slipped out while their backs were turned.

'I held the glass still and let the sun concentrate on one small spot. Sure enough, after a minute, the paper began to brown and smoke. A tiny flame appeared and we blew gently as I dropped bits of matting on it. Gradually I added splinters, then pieces of broken chair until there was a good blaze going and the walls were smouldering.

'We raced up the stairs to the open
front door – to freedom. But as we were
about to leap out into the blue daylight,
the doorway darkened. It was blocked
by an enormous man standing there with
folded arms.

'As I gazed up into the man's cold hard face, I saw only one eye looking back at me.'

'The man you dug out of the rubble!' cried Jack.

Tashi nodded. 'The muscles in his arms were hard as steel. His hand reached down to his belt and pulled out a silver dagger. I forced my gaze away from the dagger and stared straight up into his fierce snapping eye. I clenched my jaw and said quietly, "Now, sir, I *do* need my reward."

'We glared at each other for a long moment. Wang was whimpering behind me. I saw the man's eye glitter. And then he stepped aside and motioned for us to pass.

'"My debt is paid," he said.

'We raced past him and out into the cool fresh air, never stopping until we were back amongst the bustling crowds.

'Wang thanked me again and again and
wanted me to come home with him, but
I heard the clock striking the hours. Four
o'clock. I looked about. Yes, there was
the clock tower, and now I remembered –
the music box stall was close by it.
I quickly told Wang that my grandmother
would be waiting for me, and ran off.

'Keeping the tall tower in sight, I wove my way through the streets, and sure enough, I found Grandma beside the stall, peering anxiously at the passing people.

'"Oh, there you are at last, Tashi! Fancy leaving me to carry these heavy parcels by myself."

'"Sorry, Grandma," I said. I took her bags and hugged her. "I was held up."'

The boys sat in the quiet of the lift and then Jack said, 'I know how Wang felt, though.'

'What do you mean?'

'Well, what he said about being together. When you're stuck in a tight spot, it seems much less scary with two of you.'

Tashi nodded and together they looked at the great steel doors.

'But I'm still busting,' Jack confided. 'Do you need to go?'

'No,' Tashi shook his head. 'My mother says I'm like a camel. I can hold on practically forever. But see, there's a trick to it – you just have to train your mind and imagine you are somewhere completely different. For instance, I was still far away, thinking of what happened after our trip to the city.'

'You and Grandma went home and
had a big delicious dinner I suppose,'
said Jack. 'And before you went to bed,'
he added, a bit desperately, 'you went
to the toilet in peace.'

'Not exactly,' said Tashi. 'See it was
like this...'

ON THE WAY HOME

'Just a minute, did you hear something?'
Jack asked. 'Hold your breath.'

The two boys sat in the lift, listening.

'Nothing,' sighed Jack, cracking his
knuckles. 'We'll be trapped here forever.'

'No, it won't be long now,' said Tashi.
'I can feel it in my bones.'

'Which ones?'

'My left leg. It sort of tingles, deep in
my kneebone, when something's about
to happen.'

'Did it tingle like that on the way
home from the city?'

'Oh yes,' said Tashi, 'but not until dark fell. You see, while I was being kidnapped, Grandma had been very busy shopping. "Oh Tashi," she cried. "This city is such a treasure chest!" She was tired – there was city dust caked into her frown lines – but her eyes were gleaming with happiness.

'"We should be starting for home now, Grandma," I said, noticing how low the sun sat in the sky. "You know the road through the forest is lonely and famous for brigands."

'"Yes, yes," she agreed, "but just look at these presents, quick, before we go."

'You should have seen the things Grandma had bought. She'd found a wonderful shop with musical instruments and, with the money she had been saving just for me, she'd bought a silver flute. We kept opening and reopening our parcels,

forgetting about the time, listening to the
music boxes and trying out the flute, and
the ivory combs in Grandma's hair.

'At last, seeing our shadows long on
the ground, we loaded our shopping into
the cart and climbed in after it. Grandma
passed me a flaky bun and clicked her
tongue at Plodalong who snorted and
slowly moved off.

'The smells and sounds of the city faded, and soon there was only the noise of our wheels creaking over the dirt. We went quite a way in silence, and I watched the trees turning inky-black against the sky. Grandma flicked for Plodalong to quicken his pace, and he did, for a few steps.

'"He's not as frisky as he used to be," said Grandma, and I smiled at the thought of Plodalong ever being frisky. It seemed the effort was too much for him because he stumbled and slowed down even more.

'"We'll never get home before dark," Grandma fretted. "Perhaps we should stay the night at the inn up ahead."

'The inn didn't look very inviting. An unkempt fellow with his shirt buttoned up the wrong way opened the door, and I was even less happy to go in. The man looked like a brigand, but Grandma was already asking for two beds for the night. The brigand (I was quite right) waved us into a large room with some bare tables and a few hard chairs.

'"Make yourselves comfortable, please do," he grinned. "Some tea for our guests, Fearless," he growled to one of his companions.

'"Right away, Ferocious," the other replied.

'"Those are unusual names, sir," remarked Grandma mildly.

'"They are well-earned, madam," smirked Ferocious.

'"And you, sir, what is your name?" Grandma turned to the third man who slouched in the doorway, drinking something dark from a bottle.

'"He hasn't earned his name yet,"
growled Fearless. "We call him No
Name."

'"I see." Grandma introduced herself as
she sat down on one of the hard chairs.
But the two brigands weren't paying any
attention. They were discussing the
ransom money they were going to ask
for us, their guests!

'"Excuse me," said Grandma, "we
couldn't help overhearing. I can't believe
you would be so cruel to us. We have
never done you any harm."

'The brigands looked surprised and
shuffled their feet.

'"In any case," Grandma went on, "I'm afraid you'll not find anyone in our village with the money to pay a ransom for Tashi and me." And when we told them the name of our village, they agreed that no one there ever had two coins to rub together.

'But Ferocious had pricked up his ears at my name. He stared at me, nodding slightly, and as he stroked his hairy chin I saw mushed bits of noodle and prawn fall from his whiskers. I tried not to breathe in his smell of old swamp water. "There's one person in your village with money," he said, his eyes sharpening. "And from what I hear, he would pay a tidy sum to be rid of you, young Tashi."

'I breathed out in such a burst of annoyance that I nearly choked. The Baron! How I hated that man. He was so greedy and rich, of course his fame would

have spread amongst villains like
Ferocious: cruel, heartless men, with only
money on their minds. I closed my eyes
for a moment and thought. "Ah, so,"
I said, yawning a bit, giving myself time,
"it seems you have not also heard that
I have magic powers? It's well known that
if anyone tries to hurt me, my touch can
turn them to stone."

'The men jeered uneasily.

'"Very well," I said, "try me."

'Ferocious and Fearless began to mutter together in a huddle. Still clutching his wine bottle, No Name made his way across the room towards them. He swayed on his feet, stopping now and then to get his balance.

'As I peered into the smoky candlelight,
I noticed how different he seemed from
the other two – with his old silk waistcoat
and his beard braided into two dusty
plaits. He caught my eye and gave a
nervous shiver, like an animal whose fur
has been stroked the wrong way.

43

'"Come here and pay *attention*," Ferocious spat at him. There was a little more muttering and then Ferocious clapped Fearless on the back. "*I* know," he said in a loud whisper. "There's more than one way to skin a cat," and with a quick glance at me, "or a boy." He pulled Fearless aside. "We'll wait till he's asleep and then No Name can creep into his room and finish him off in the usual way."

'*The usual way?* I didn't like the sound of that. "Why me?" complained No Name, pulling frantically at his plaited beard.

'So I was ready when the door opened quietly that night. I was hiding behind a cupboard and watched grimly while No Name tip-toed (*he* didn't want to be turned to stone) into the room. He wasn't swaying on his feet now, but I saw his hands tremble as he pulled a pistol from

his belt and pointed it at the bump in the
bed clothes. "The Gods forgive me,"
he moaned as he pulled the trigger.

'BANG! Had he missed? No Name
edged further into the room. No he hadn't:
a red stain was seeping through the sheets.
Mumbling to himself he staggered out of
the room, leaving me to clean up the ripe
tomatoes I had thoughtfully settled on the
pillow and under the bedclothes.

'The next morning I bounced into the kitchen. "Mmn, that smells good."

'The brigands dropped their chopsticks and stared. They hurried to fill my bowl with rice porridge before they dragged No Name away into the far corner. "I did, I *did*," I heard him protesting.

'"Well, we'll have to do something quickly," Ferocious hissed. "Blackheart is coming tomorrow and he won't want to find unfinished business here." Ferocious was twisting his shirt buttons. No Name grew so pale he looked as if he might pass out.

'In the early evening when the robbers were preparing dinner, Fearless whispered to No Name, "Have you got it?" No Name nodded and slipped a paper cone into his hand. I was on my guard at once.

'Fearless poured the soup into the bowls and sure enough, I saw that some powder was tipped into mine. I jumped up and made a fuss about helping Grandma to her chair and collecting her soup, and in the confusion I swapped Ferocious's bowl with mine.

'That night I smiled to myself as I heard groans and curses ("You could have killed me!") from the brigands' room. I wasn't surprised when, just after dawn, I learned that Ferocious was feeling poorly and didn't want breakfast.

'All morning Fearless and No Name grew more and more agitated as they waited for Blackheart to arrive. There were three wine bottles lined up on the great table and they were nearly empty. No Name paced up and down, tapping the bottles with his chopsticks, making a tune.

'"If you don't stop that," Fearless finally shouted, "I'll cut off your piddling plaits and stuff them up your noseholes!"

'No Name sank onto a chair. He rocked himself and stared at the floor. When Ferocious came in, holding his stomach, I moved closer to hear snatches of their conversation.

'"Everything hurts," Ferocious groaned, and closed his eyes.

'"But what will Blackheart say about the boy?" whined Fearless. "You know what he does to people who..."

'"How were *we* to know?"

'"A boy who turns people to *stone*..."

'A feeling of dread stole over me, too. It was cold and clammy, like the hand of a ghost, and it reached inside and twisted my stomach. Blackheart, I was sure, would not be so easy to trick.

'By the time we heard a horse approaching the inn, No Name was rocking wildly, wringing his hands. Grandma got up from the chair. "If you're quick," she whispered to him, "you could just let us go. Blackheart need never know we were here."

'"That's right," I agreed. "We'll slip out. There's still time."

'"It's no use," wailed No Name. "He would find out. He always does. Here, boy," he turned to me, "hide under the table while I think."

'The door flew open.

'"Why was no one ready to take my horse?" thundered Blackheart.

'Grandma's hands flew to her face. Striding through the doorway was a giant of a man. He had the cruellest snarl of a mouth I had ever seen. This was a face that knew no pity. Blackheart didn't notice Grandma standing against the wall. He was dragging No Name outside to gather up his boxes of loot and plunder.

'While they were gone I came out from under the table. "Oh dear, now I have seen your master, I am really very sorry for you all."

'Ferocious and Fearless gaped at me. "You're sorry for *us*?"

'"Yes, he reminds me exactly of a pirate who once captured me. He was pitiless too, and when he was told that I could turn his enemies to stone at a touch, he didn't know whether to believe it or not. So do you know what he did?"

'Ferocious and Fearless looked at me uneasily. "Well, what did he do then?"

'"He made his men touch me, one by one. Slowly their limbs turned to marble, then their bodies. They cried for mercy but it was too late; their lips froze and their poor despairing eyes looked to me for help. But once touched, there was nothing I could do. You can see their marble figures to this day by the well in our village."

'Ferocious shuddered. "Quick," he said, "out you go, out the back door. Your horse and cart are down the track under the trees. We'll keep Blackheart busy until you're out of sight."

'Grandma and I slipped out and scrambled into the cart. Almost as if he knew, Plodalong set off at a smart trot, happy as we were to leave the inn behind.

'Grandma flicked the reins. "It was lucky you had that good idea, Tashi. I hope Ferocious doesn't ever come to our village looking for the marble statues."

'I laughed. "I don't think he will. In any case, I've already made up a good reason for them being gone."

'Grandma tweaked my ear. "What a clever Tashi!"

Jack grinned at his friend. '*Did* you ever see the brigands again?'

'Only No Name. But he wasn't a brigand anymore when I spotted him.'

'What was he doing?'

'Juggling firesticks on a high wire.'

Jack's mouth fell open in surprise. 'Didn't he fall off?'

Tashi shook his head. 'No, he'd given up the drink. Said he didn't need it now that he was doing what he'd always loved best.'

'What, balancing on a high wire?'

'That's right. He was once a travelling acrobat, you see, and he'd left home very young to see the world. But it wasn't long before he got lost in the city, just like I did, and he fell in with thieves and brigands.'

In the thoughtful silence, the two boys gazed at the lift doors.

'Of course, as Grandma says, *some* people never climb out of the dark pit of greed and selfishness.'

'No,' agreed Jack. 'Like that Blackheart.'

'Or Bluebeard,' Tashi said grimly.

Jack swung around to face Tashi. 'Who?'

Tashi shivered. 'When I met Bluebeard, all the other evil men I'd ever met seemed *gentle* in comparison.'

Just then the floor underneath the two boys shuddered. Their stomachs lurched as the lift began to drop like a stone.

'What's happening?' cried Jack.

The lift stopped suddenly, with a loud jarring thump. The boys clutched each other, breathing fast.

Then a voice came from the other side.

'Hullo? Anyone in there?'

'YES, *YES*, we're here!'

'Just a jiffy and we'll get you out,' called the cheerful voice. 'Only a few more minutes...'

Jack and Tashi looked at each other.

Jack squirmed. He squeezed his legs together hard. 'So, tell me, how did you meet Bluebeard?'

But Tashi sprang up and began hopping about. 'It was too terrible to talk about now. To tell you the truth, Jack, I'm really busting, too. I'll...I'll tell you on the way home.'

And at that moment the great steel doors opened and a ginger-haired man stepped through with a big smile. But the boys flew past him like streamers in the wind and headed straight for the sign...